Dear Parents:

Congratulations! Your child is taking the first steps on an exciting journey. The destination? Independent reading!

STEP INTO READING® will help your child get there. The program offers five steps to reading success. Each step includes fun stories and colorful art or photographs. In addition to original fiction and books with favorite characters, there are Step into Reading Non-Fiction Readers, Phonics Readers and Boxed Sets, Sticker Readers, and Comic Readers—a complete literacy program with something to interest every child.

Learning to Read, Step by Step!

Ready to Read   Preschool–Kindergarten
• big type and easy words • rhyme and rhythm • picture clues
For children who know the alphabet and are eager to begin reading.

Reading with Help   Preschool–Grade 1
• basic vocabulary • short sentences • simple stories
For children who recognize familiar words and sound out new words with help.

Reading on Your Own   Grades 1–3
• engaging characters • easy-to-follow plots • popular topics
For children who are ready to read on their own.

Reading Paragraphs   Grades 2–3
• challenging vocabulary • short paragraphs • exciting stories
For newly independent readers who read simple sentences with confidence.

Ready for Chapters   Grades 2–4
• chapters • longer paragraphs • full-color art
For children who want to take the plunge into chapter books but still like colorful pictures.

STEP INTO READING® is designed to give every child a successful reading experience. The grade levels are only guides; children will progress through the steps at their own speed, developing confidence in their reading.

Remember, a lifetime love of reading starts with a single step!

For my brilliant Dash & jolly Otter,
the two special party animals who lit up my life —S.L.

To M.B.—the Pokey to my Grumpy Cat —F.B.

grumpycats.com

Visit us on the Web!
StepIntoReading.com
rhcbooks.com

Educators and librarians, for a variety of teaching tools, visit us at
RHTeachersLibrarians.com

ISBN 978-1-9848-5030-0 (trade) — ISBN 978-1-9848-5031-7 (lib. bdg.) —
ISBN 978-1-9848-5032-4 (ebook)

Printed in the United States of America

10 9 8 7 6 5 4 3 2

Grumpy Cat®
UNHAPPY BIRTHDAY, GRUMPY CAT!

by Frank Berrios
illustrated by Steph Laberis

Random House 🏠 New York

Pokey is excited.

Today is a
very special day!

He is planning
a surprise party
for Grumpy Cat!

Oh, no!
Grumpy Cat
spots the balloons
and presents.
She is not happy.

"Surprise, Grumpy Cat!"
her friends cheer.
They put on
their party hats.

"Ow! Too tight!"
says Grumpy Cat.

It is time for some
party games!
Yay!

Grumpy Cat frowns.
A sack race?
"I would rather not,"
she says.

"Grumpy Cat,
look at all
of your presents!"
says Pokey.

"I hate the noisy
wrapping paper,"
grumbles Grumpy Cat.

Pokey loves
the colorful ribbons.
"This is fun!"
he says.

Grumpy Cat
gets tangled up.
"This is *not* fun!"
she says.

It is time to sing
"Happy Birthday"
to Grumpy Cat.

"Too loud!"
shouts Grumpy Cat.

The friends love
the birthday cake.

Grumpy Cat thinks
the cake is too sweet.

What a busy day.
Now it is time
to clean up.

Grumpy Cat and Pokey
say goodbye
to their friends.
"Finally!"
mumbles Grumpy Cat.

Pokey and Grumpy Cat
get ready for bed.
"Did you have
a good birthday?"
asks Pokey.

"The best part was when
everyone left,"
says Grumpy Cat.